Contents

ENGLAND

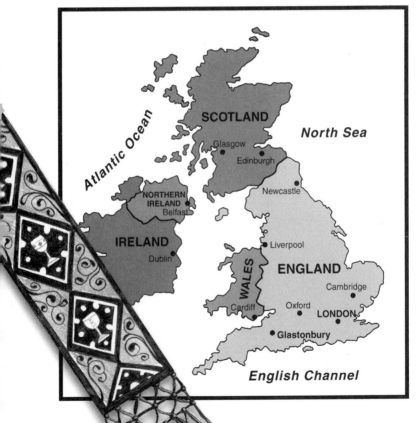

QUEST for the CUP

by Katrina O'Neill and Lisa Thompson
illustrated by Brenda Cantell

TM
sundance
A Haights Cross Communications Company

Published by Sundance Publishing
One Beeman Road
P.O. Box 740
Northborough, MA 01532-0740
800-343-8204
www.sundancepub.com

Copyright © text Katrina O'Neill and Lisa Thompson
Copyright © illustrations Brenda Cantell

First published as Treasure Trackers by
Blake Education, Locked Bag 2022, Glebe 2037, Australia
Exclusive United States Distribution: Sundance Publishing

ISBN 0-7608-9332-2

GLASTONBURY ABBEY

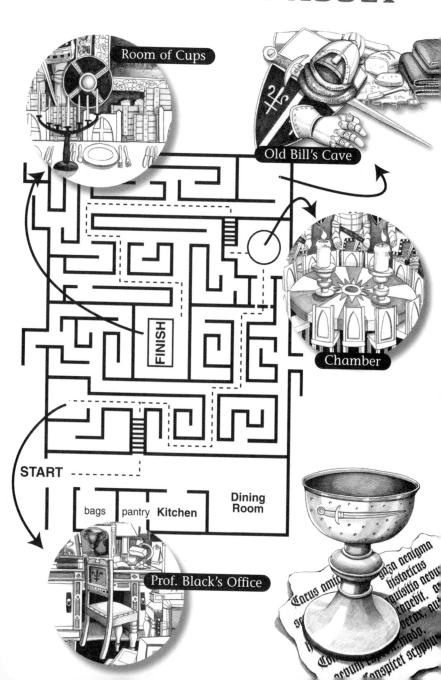

Room of Cups

Old Bill's Cave

Chamber

FINISH

START

bags pantry **Kitchen**

Dining Room

Prof. Black's Office

CHAPTER 1

To the Abbey

Heavy thumps and loud crashes filled the
darkness. The strange noises jolted Ricky awake.
Mia was already up looking for her flashlight.

"Burglars!" whispered Mia. "Come on, Ricky.
They're in Uncle Earl's study." As they crept
down the hallway, Mia grabbed a carved spear
from the wall.

"We're being ro . . . robbed!" stammered Ricky,
helping himself to an ancient Chinese sword.

They stood on either side of the study door,
listening to the heavy footsteps coming from
within. A strip of light shone beneath the door.

"It sounds like they're ripping the place apart!" whispered Ricky.

Mia raised her spear. "OK, Ricky, on the count of three, you fling open the door. Ready?"

Ricky gripped his sword and nodded.

Mia mouthed, "One . . . two . . . three!" They threw the door wide open and leaped inside with bloodcurdling screams.

"Drop everything NOW!" demanded Mia, holding her spear high in the air.

Uncle Earl was standing at the top of a ladder
leaning against a bookshelf. As he turned,
startled, he dropped a small box. There was a
loud crash as it landed on the floor. Uncle Earl
raised his arms in surrender. Mia and Ricky
stared at the floor of the study. It was a gigantic
mess of books, papers, folders, videos, cassettes,
and overflowing boxes.

"Uncle Earl!" cried Mia, putting down the spear.
"What are you doing?"

Ricky picked up a box from the pile. "Looking for something, Uncle Earl?"

"We thought you were an intruder," explained Mia. "We thought we were being robbed. What on earth are you looking for?"

"A photo," said Uncle Earl, as he descended the ladder and started sorting through the mess. "A very special photo of my friend Professor Black and myself, taken many years ago in Rome. I saw it just the other day, and for the life of me, I don't know where I put it. It's here somewhere. It's got to be."

"Well, there can't be too many places left to pull apart," said Ricky, scanning the room.

Mia laughed as she held up a plastic bag marked *Rare white rhino toenail clippings.* Her uncle kept the strangest things! "Why do you need this photo right now? I mean, it's five o'clock in the morning! Can't it wait?"

Ricky held up an old, faded photograph of two men eating pizza. He had found it sticking out of the top of a book. "Is this it?" he asked.

"Yes, that's it!" Uncle Earl took the photograph and held it in the light. "Well done, Ricky. I must have used it as a bookmark the other day when I was reading."

Mia and Ricky looked at the photograph to see what all the fuss was about. Uncle Earl looked very young and had a head full of curly hair. The other man was thin and wore a beaming smile. They were both sitting at a café table with a glass of soda in one hand and a slice of pizza in the other.

"You look different with all that hair, Uncle Earl," giggled Mia.

"What an awful sweater," laughed Ricky.

"I'll have you know that I was very fashionable in those days, my boy," Uncle Earl said.

"Professor Black is going to get a real kick out of seeing this photo this afternoon."

"But we're spending the day going through ancient Chinese artifacts," said Mia. "When will we be seeing him?"

"Change of plans," declared Uncle Earl as he lifted a pile of papers to find his watch. "I had a call from Professor Black late last night. We're all booked on a flight to London. It leaves in about three hours."

"London?" gasped Mia. "Cool! I've always wanted to go to England." She rushed back to her room to pack.

Ricky was less impressed. "Why is it always rush, rush, rush?" he muttered to himself. "No one in this treasure-tracking business seems to sleep. Everyone wants their treasure yesterday. People NEED sleep, you know." He dragged himself down the hall, mumbling, "I was having such a good dream. I was just about to unearth the biggest treasure of my life." He fell on his bed and pulled up the covers.

"Well, get up and maybe you will get the chance to find it for real," said Mia sternly. "England's full of castles and ancient treasure. It's treasure-tracker heaven!"

"I wonder if you get to sleep in heaven," yawned Ricky.

"You'll have plenty of time to sleep on the plane. Now, where did you leave your passport?"

On the plane, Uncle Earl and Ricky went straight to sleep. Mia, on the other hand, was wide-awake. Uncle Earl hadn't told them what kind of treasure they would be looking for in England. Mia's mind was racing fast. Was it crown jewels . . . precious gems . . . priceless artwork . . . royal heirlooms? Mia knew it had to be something very important for Uncle Earl to be called in. People always turned to him when they thought they might be on the verge of discovering something big but couldn't quite find it on their own.

Light rain drizzled down, and it was cold and gloomy when they walked out of Heathrow Airport. Professor Black had arranged for a car to meet them.

"Wonderful weather we're having!" joked the driver pleasantly.

"Indeed!" said Uncle Earl, climbing into the back of the car with Ricky and Mia. Ricky wiped off the window so he could see out, while Mia studied a map of England.

"Better not keep Professor Black waiting," said the driver, picking up speed. "I've never seen a man so eager to see people."

Mia couldn't hold back her questions a second longer. "OK, Uncle Earl, do you mind telling us where we are headed and why?"

Uncle Earl smiled. "We're on our way to Glastonbury." He lowered his voice so the driver couldn't hear. "Professor Black thinks he has found a clue that will lead us to the Holy Grail."

Mia dropped her map. "Really?"

Ricky looked confused. "I thought that the Holy Grail was just a legend—a story. Besides, isn't it just a cup? It doesn't sound like much of a treasure to me."

"Ricky, many a treasure has been found because of a story," said Uncle Earl. "Anyway, the legend says that King Arthur sent his Knights on a quest to recover the Holy Grail. The Grail was said to bring good fortune to whoever possessed it. People have been searching for it for centuries. I tell you, if we do find it, it will be one of the greatest finds of all time."

"Isn't there a theory that the cup is hidden in a well on the hill behind the cemetery at Glastonbury?" asked Mia.

Uncle Earl nodded. "There are many theories when it comes to the Grail, Mia. And yes, that is one of them. It will be interesting to see what new information Professor Black has for us. He has been working with the monks from the Abbey at Glastonbury for years now."

"Man, it's cold," said Ricky, pulling the hood of
his sweatshirt over his head and the sleeves over
his hands.

"Better not walk around the Abbey like that,
Ricky. You may be mistaken for a monk!"
chuckled Uncle Earl.

"How do you know Professor Black?" asked Mia.

"We studied Latin in Italy together. It was Professor Black who got me interested in the Grail. That photo Ricky found this morning was taken on the day we first talked about it. Professor Black vowed to me that he would be the one to find the cup. He used to keep me entertained for hours with medieval stories about King Arthur and the Grail Knights."

They had reached the highway that would take them to Glastonbury. Uncle Earl closed his eyes and nodded off to sleep again. Mia circled the places they passed on her map. Ricky gazed out the window and imagined himself at King Arthur's table.

"We're here," announced the driver. "Welcome to Glastonbury Abbey."

CHAPTER 2

A Clue in Stitches

Professor Black ran to the car to greet them. He still had the same wide grin. "Earl! I'm so grateful that you could come so quickly."

"Hello, Mia, and you must be Ricky," he said as he shook their hands. He leaned closer to them and whispered, "I guess you're used to this kind of grab-and-run travel." He smiled. "Let's take your things inside and get started, shall we?" They unloaded the car and walked up the steps of the Abbey.

"Oh, just one thing," said Professor Black. "You should keep the reason why you are here a secret. If anyone asks, just say you're here to help me with research. I haven't told the monks anything about what I think I've discovered. Most of them are on a three-month vow of silence, so I thought it best to wait and see."

"No speaking for three months?" laughed Ricky. "Uncle Earl, can we sign Mia up for that? Hey Mia, I dare you to take the challenge!"

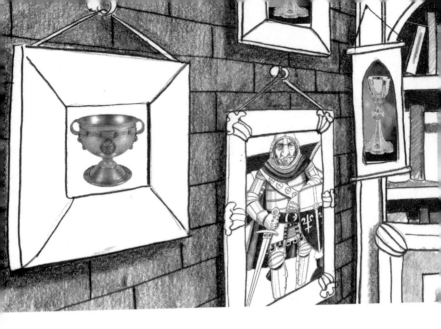

The Abbey seemed deserted and eerily quiet.
"The monks spend this part of the day at work,"
explained Professor Black. He showed them a
room where they could leave their bags. Then
they followed him down some narrow, steep
stone stairs. At the bottom of the stairs, they
took a left turn and walked down a long
hallway until they came to a solid wooden door.
"This is where I have been doing most of my
research," explained Professor Black.

The small room was filled with piles of old books
and paintings of knights and ancient cups. The
only light came from a dim desk lamp.

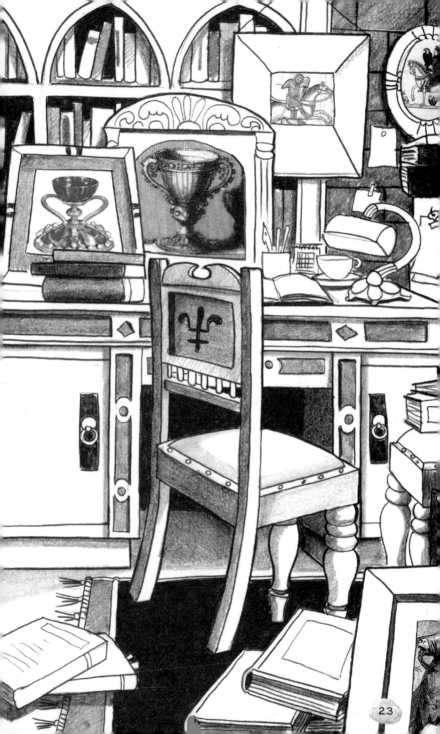

Professor Black opened a secret compartment under his desk. He took out an old and very beautiful tapestry.

"Superb!" murmured Uncle Earl, as it was unrolled. "Where on earth did you find it?"

"Below the Abbey is a maze of passageways. I've been trying to map them all. Two days ago, I found a new passage. I could tell that no one had been down it for a very long time. The passage led me to a small chamber. None of the books about the Abbey mention this chamber. I doubt if the monks even know that it exists," said the professor with growing excitement.

He took a deep breath and continued, "There were some old chairs and a table in the chamber. As I sat down on one of the chairs, the seat gave way. I almost fell through it! I couldn't believe my luck when I found this tapestry hidden inside. I'm sure that it holds a clue to the whereabouts of the Grail."

Uncle Earl studied the ancient tapestry. He mumbled to himself as he read the text. The central picture was of a knight on a horse following a glowing cup.

"What does it say, Uncle Earl?" asked Mia. "Does it talk of the Grail?"

Uncle Earl nodded and smiled. "Yes, it definitely does! This is very impressive. It seems to talk of the resting place of the Grail, but it also seems to be full of riddles. Have you begun to decipher this?" he asked, turning to Professor Black.

Professor Black smiled. "Not yet, old friend. I thought this is an adventure we could begin together."

Uncle Earl pulled out the photograph from his jacket and gave it to Professor Black. "This seems like the right time to show you this."

"Oh, my!" he said softly. "Look at us! That was the day we first talked about the Grail. It marks the start of a quest I've been on ever since."

"So let's see if this tapestry leads us to the cup," said Uncle Earl.

CHAPTER 3

Empty or Full?

While Uncle Earl and Professor Black discussed how they would proceed, Mia and Ricky looked at the books and paintings around the room.

"There must be thousands of images of the Grail here," declared Mia. "Yet all of them look different. How do you know which one is the right one?"

"If you found the real cup you'd know, Mia," answered Professor Black. He handed Mia one of his personal notebooks and pointed to some text. "This is how the legends say you can identify the Grail."

Mia read the paragraph to Ricky.

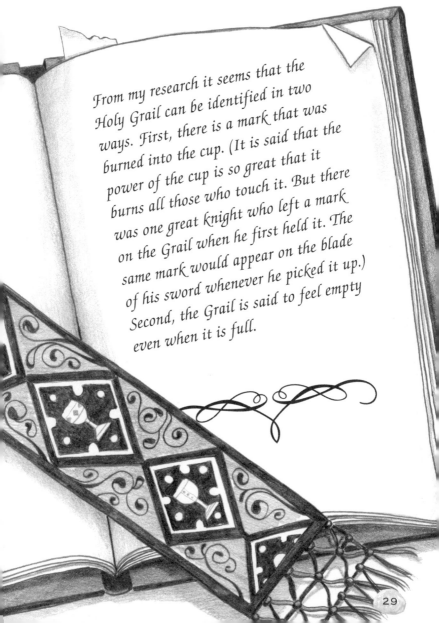

From my research it seems that the Holy Grail can be identified in two ways. First, there is a mark that was burned into the cup. (It is said that the power of the cup is so great that it burns all those who touch it. But there was one great knight who left a mark on the Grail when he first held it. The same mark would appear on the blade of his sword whenever he picked it up.) Second, the Grail is said to feel empty even when it is full.

Ricky just shrugged. He was more interested in the pictures of knights locked in battle. Mia, on the other hand, was fascinated. It seemed that the more she found out about the Grail, the more mysterious it became.

Hours passed, and still Uncle Earl and Professor Black were engrossed in their work.

"Hey, Professor, would you mind if Mia and I found something to eat?" asked Ricky, rubbing his rumbling stomach.

"I'm sorry. I should have offered you something earlier. I'm afraid I'm thinking only of the cup. Why don't you go upstairs to the kitchen? You'll find it just down the hall from where we left your bags."

"Thanks," said Ricky, dragging Mia away.

"But . . ." she protested.

"Mia," whispered Ricky, "I'm sure your sharp eyes could find a few new clues around this place. I say we do a little exploring on our own."

They found the kitchen and made themselves sandwiches. Two monks were working silently in the kitchen pantry.

Ricky found a quiet spot where he and Mia could sit. He pulled a sheet of paper from his pocket. "Have a look at what I found in the professor's office. It's a map of the Abbey and all of the passageways he has discovered so far. It shows the way to the chamber. I say we go find this room that Professor Black talked about."

"Ricky!" Mia was shocked and grabbed the map. "He'll be looking for this!"

"No way. You saw how much work he and Uncle Earl have to do. They won't be looking at anything else for days."

Mia studied the map, and then she nodded. "We'd better grab the flashlights I packed." She traced a path on the map. "We can go in this way." She gave a determined smile. "Let's go."

They went down the same stone stairs but turned right at the bottom this time. Mia handed Ricky a piece of paper and a pencil. "I know we've got the map, but we should still write down the turns we make. That way we can double-check if we get lost. Every time we make a turn, write down which way we go."

Ricky nodded. He had to hand it to Mia—no matter what the circumstances were, she always managed to think of everything.

They walked down the dark, stone passageway, waving their flashlights through the darkness. Ricky kept track of their directions—right, left, left, right, left, right. It certainly was a maze. Sometimes one passageway would branch in three different directions. At other times, a passageway became so narrow they could barely fit through. Professor Black was right about one thing. It sure looked as if no one had been down there in a very, very long time.

"This place is creepy," muttered Ricky, wriggling through yet another tight spot.

Mia stopped and held up her flashlight. "Oh, no!" she groaned.

"What?" said Ricky catching up.

"It's a dead end."

Ricky looked at the map. "It can't be. According to the map, there should be another small room that leads into the chamber. Look."

"Yeah, I know what the map says, but we happen to be staring at a stone wall," said Mia despondently.

"There has to be a door," said Ricky, running his hands over the wall. "Maybe there's a secret opening."

CHAPTER 4

Candles in the Wind

Mia knelt on the ground and felt along the bottom of the wall. She could feel cracks in the wall and then saw a footprint carved in the stone floor.

"Look, Ricky. There's something here. I think that it might be a very low door. Push on this part of the rock with me." They pushed with all their strength, and the rock slid back. There was just enough space for them to crawl through.

"Professor Black didn't mention anything about this," Ricky puffed. They found themselves in a small room. There was a dim, flickering light coming through another doorway.

Mia whispered, "That must be the chamber. I guess that's candlelight." Mia paused. "Do you think someone else is here?"

"I don't know. Maybe that's how the professor left it," said Ricky nervously.

"Let's hope so," she answered, edging forward. "Only one way to find out."

"It looks like no one is here," said Mia softly.

In the middle of the room was an imposing, round, wooden table. Two large candles sitting on the table lit the entire chamber, and twelve suits of battle armor hung on the walls. Everything seemed in eerily perfect order.

As Mia turned to survey the rest of the room, she noticed a crest, with a symbol of a cup, above the entrance. She walked across to examine it more closely.

39

Ricky walked eagerly toward one of the suits.
"Hey, Mia, check this out."

Suddenly, the candles flickered and went out.
Mia and Ricky stood silently in the darkness
until Mia turned on her flashlight.

"Probably just the wind," she said weakly.

"I didn't notice any wind," said Ricky, flicking
on his flashlight, too. "I'll check the door."

Ricky went back into the small room and flashed his light over the entrance. "It's OK, Mia. We're not stuck in here." He waited for her answer. "Mia! I said it's OK," Ricky called as he walked back toward the chamber. "Mia!" he called again.

As his flashlight scanned the room, he could see that the chamber was empty. He checked the walls and the floor for gaps or marks, but there was nothing. Mia had vanished!

Chapter 5

The Grail Knight

"Come on, Mia. This isn't funny. I'm the one who plays the tricks. Come out, will you?" Ricky pleaded as he searched under the large table. It was then that he noticed, lying on the floor, a sword that had been attached to one of the suits of armor. Ricky picked up the sword and walked over to the suit of armor. He stopped, stunned. The armor hid an entrance to another set of stone stairs.

He pushed the armor aside and yelled into the dark stairwell, "Mia, are you down there?" His voice echoed, but there was no reply. He shone the flashlight into the darkness as he started down the stairs.

The air was stagnant, and the steps were wet and slippery. At the bottom of the stairs were three icy-cold passageways. There was no sign of Mia. However, Ricky could hear a faint sound, like a voice, coming from the passage to the right, so he took that path.

He crept along slowly with his heart beating hard in his chest. "Mia, I hope that's you in there," he muttered to himself when he saw a light coming from the end of the passageway.

43

"Mia," he yelled as he entered, "what's the big idea running off? We're supposed to be doing this together."

"She's not here," said an old man dressed in tattered clothes. He was tending a fire in the corner. "My bet is she's gone after the Grail. She couldn't wait—that's what happens to people. Now she's on a quest of her own."

Ricky stood staring at the man. "Who . . . who are you?" he stammered. "Are you looking for the Grail, too?"

"One question at a time, my lad." The old man smiled. "Come closer to the fire. Don't worry, I won't bite."

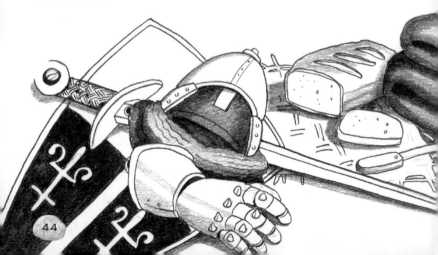

"So you want to know if I'm after the Grail, too? My boy, let me tell you a little secret—everyone's after it in their own way. Life is just one big quest," he sighed. "Trouble is, most people don't know what they're looking for."

He handed Ricky a warm drink. Ricky hesitated before he took it.

"It won't hurt you. It's tea. I just boiled the water. It'll warm you up."

Ricky took a sip and edged closer to the fire. He hadn't realized how cold he was. "Thanks. Have you seen my friend, Mia?"

"No, can't say I have. You're the first person I've seen down here in a long, long time. I did hear someone come down those stairs not long before you. No one came in here, but it sounded like the person was in a hurry and knew exactly where to go."

Ricky looked around the cave. It was empty except for blankets, bread, a few candles, and some old knight's armor and sword. The old man followed Ricky's gaze and, moving away from the fire, picked up the sword.

"Would you like to hold it?" he asked quietly.

Ricky nodded. As the old man's hands left the blade of the sword, Ricky's eyes widened, and he gasped. The old man had left a mark on the blade that slowly faded away after a few seconds. Ricky couldn't believe his eyes.

"Are you a Grail Knight?" Ricky blurted out.

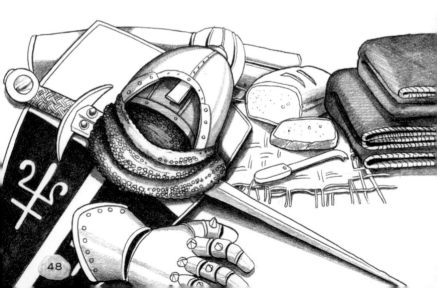

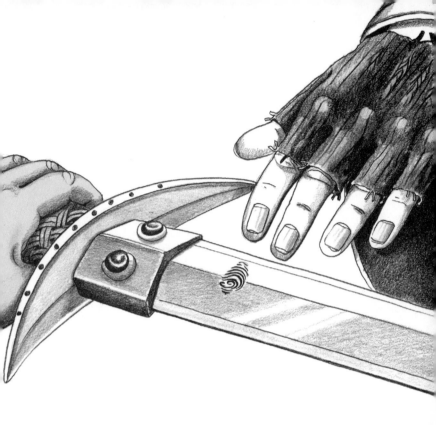

The old man gave a hearty laugh. "My boy, if you're searching for something that means the world to you, and you search long enough and hard enough, then you are a Grail Knight. Like I said before, we're all searching. It's just that some of us don't know it. The main thing you must remember is that you have to really believe in what you're looking for. That's what keeps you going."

He shook Ricky's hand. "The name's Old Bill. I've been around these passages for so long that time doesn't mean a thing. It's the Grail that brought me down here, and it's the Grail that keeps me here." He stoked the fire. "More tea?"

"Ah, no thanks," said Ricky getting up. "I really should get back to looking for Mia. She could be back in the chamber waiting for me."

"Not much chance of that," sighed Old Bill. "Once you get that Grail idea in your head, it's pretty hard to think about anything else. If I were you, and I wanted to find her, I'd start thinking like her. That's the key. Looking for the cup does strange things to you. You can get really lost, or worse still, you can get charmed by it." He gave a little laugh and sat down again in front of the fire. "I guess that is its power. It's a beautiful thing, the Grail."

"So you've seen it! Have you held it?" asked Ricky.

Old Bill didn't answer. He just gazed into the fire.

"Well, thanks for the tea, Old Bill," Ricky said, moving toward the door.

"That's all right," Old Bill replied. "Just do me a favor, and don't tell anyone you saw me. The last thing I need is a bunch of people disturbing my peace. The Grail does enough of that already," he laughed. "Think like Mia would. That's the only way you're going to find her now. Otherwise, you could lose her for good."

CHAPTER 6

Mia's Quest

Mia could hardly believe it when the suit of armor moved forward, and the staircase was revealed. She couldn't think of anything but the cup. She didn't even think to wait for Ricky.

As Mia squeezed past the armor, she brushed the sword and heard it hit the ground. She didn't stop to look—she just kept going. She was in a hurry. At the bottom of the stairs, she took the left passageway, certain that the cup wasn't far away.

She hurried along the passageways, not thinking about what she had left behind.

Her thoughts were only on what she was about to discover.

Turn after turn revealed nothing, but all of Mia's instincts urged her forward. With each empty passageway, she said to herself, "That's OK. It'll be in the next one." Mia only stopped when she came to an enormous, high-ceilinged room lined with wooden crates.

The room also had a wooden table, but this
table was rectangular and set for a formal
dinner. The walls were lined with mirrors and
tapestries showing knights dressed in full armor.
There were large, battered coats of arms. Suits of
armor with swords hung from the ceiling.

Mia hung her flashlight from one of the swords
to light up the room. Nothing she saw made
any impression on her. She was after only one
treasure, only one cup—the Grail.

"It has to be here somewhere," she shouted.

Mia began to open the crates. Each one was filled with different cups and goblets. As she took a cup from its crate, she would place it on the table. Soon there were hundreds of cups crowding against each other. Some were quite plain, while others were covered in sparkling jewels and gold.

Professor Black's notes came back to Mia.
"*. . . there was one great knight . . . left a mark on the Grail . . . said to feel empty even when it is full.*"

Mia began the huge task of examining each cup to see if it was the Grail. While every one was beautiful in its own way, none had a mark resembling a fingerprint, and while some were heavy, they all felt empty.

"I wish Ricky was here to help," sighed Mia. It was only then that she realized what she had done. She had left her best friend behind! Her mind had been completely taken over by her quest for the Grail.

"I'll have to go back," she whispered. "But I can't. I don't know the way."

Mia suddenly knew that her quest for the cup had left her lost and alone.

CHAPTER 7

Ricky's Quest

Ricky spoke to himself as he stood at the bottom of the stone stairs, "So, Old Bill says I have to think like Mia." He pondered for a moment. "Well, she always thinks the opposite of me. She says I think all over the place. Mia loves order." He started to laugh. "In fact, her mind works as though it's marching. I bet it would go *left, left, left, right, left,*" Ricky pretended to march on the spot. "That's it. Mia's brain would go left just because I'd want to go right."

Ricky took a deep breath and walked forward, flashlight in hand. The passageway narrowed and the walls began to close in on him. Ricky had to fight the feeling of wanting to run back.

He started to wonder if he'd really seen Old Bill at all. Maybe he was going crazy.

Ricky broke into a run. As his footsteps echoed off the walls, it sounded as if he was being chased. He stopped and shook his head. He was alone. It was only the thoughts in his head that were chasing him. Ricky now called out the direction he took at every turn. "Left! Left! Right!" He wondered if he was getting any closer to finding Mia, or just further away.

He had almost given up, and was thinking about trying to find his way back, when he remembered Old Bill's words. Ricky whispered to himself, "If you want to find something, you have to really believe. I know this is the way Mia would have come. I know it." He took a deep breath and screamed, "Miaaaaaaa!" And then again, "Miaaaaaaaa!"

There was silence. Then came a faint reply, "Over here!"

"Mia! Mia, where are you?" Ricky yelled as he ran along the passageway. At the end, he had to choose between left and right. "Mia, tell me where you are!" His words echoed back to him.

Mia's call sounded shaky. "Ricky, I'm here."

"Hold on, I'm coming," he called, taking the left passage. He turned a corner, and from there, saw a faint glow up ahead. As he ran closer, he could see Mia waiting for him. "Yes!" Ricky thought triumphantly. "You were right, Old Bill. It worked!"

"I've been searching everywhere. Why did you run off without . . ."

Ricky stopped talking as he reached the room. He was stunned. There, before him, was a huge pile of beautiful cups and goblets.

"Awesome!" he gasped. "What a find! How many are there?"

Mia shrugged with weary disappointment. "Who cares?"

"What do you mean? Have you gone crazy? It's mind-blowing! This pile must be worth a fortune," gasped Ricky.

"But not one of them is what I was after. Not one of them is the Grail," Mia sighed. "Ricky, I'm sorry for leaving you alone. I don't know what happened. I just wanted to find the Grail. I didn't know the way back and . . ."

Ricky nodded. "It's OK. I understand. This whole Grail thing can make you do really strange things. Hey, do you hear that?"

Hurried footsteps were echoing up the passageway. Uncle Earl and Professor Black burst into the room.

"Mia! Ricky! How on earth . . . ?" Uncle Earl's shock at finding them here was wiped away when he saw the contents of the room. Still clutching the tapestry, he stood wide-eyed. "Remarkable!" he finally gasped. "Incredible!"

"Astonishing! Astonishing!" cried Professor Black as he picked up cup after cup.

"Forget it," sighed Mia. "I've checked them all, and not one of them is the one we're looking for. There are gold, silver, brass, jeweled, plain, big, small, carved, and engraved cups, but there's no Grail. Sorry, Professor, but it looks like the tapestry was wrong."

"No, it wasn't wrong, Mia," corrected Professor Black. "The tapestry describes a room where the Grail might be found—and this must be it! We only worked it out when Earl and I deciphered the riddles."

Ricky held up a jeweled cup. "Well, you may not have the Grail, Professor, but you certainly have found some treasure!"

"It seems we all found this treasure in our own way," Professor Black laughed.

They searched the room to make sure there was nothing else hidden from them. Professor Black almost burst with delight every time he picked up a cup. Mia began to feel less disappointed about not finding the Grail.

"Mia, never be disappointed with a find. Look how long I've been searching. One thing I've learned is that no find is a bad find because it just means you're one step closer." Professor Black smiled. "And this is a particularly MAGNIFICENT find!"

"By the way," said Uncle Earl to Mia and Ricky, "how did you two find this place? Weren't you supposed to be having lunch?"

"You know how it is, Uncle Earl. You take a different turn, and suddenly you're on your way to somewhere else," grinned Mia.

"Indeed!" agreed Uncle Earl, nodding his head and raising a cup. For a moment he looked like the young Uncle Earl from the photograph. "How right you are!"

CHAPTER 8

Old Bill's Message

Back at the Abbey, with the help of the monks, they set to work cataloging all the items from the room. Uncle Earl and Professor Black gave Ricky and Mia the job of mapping the rest of the passageways under the Abbey.

Ricky never ran into Old Bill again or the cave where he spoke to him. He kept his word and never mentioned Old Bill to anyone. Ricky did, however, find a note that he was sure had been left by Old Bill. It was hidden in one of the cups.

The cup lay in a plain, wooden box. It was engraved with a picture of a knight's sword, very similar to the one that Old Bill had shown him. Ricky picked up the cup, which to his surprise was still warm. Inside the cup was a folded note on old parchment. It was written in Latin. Ricky gave it to Mia's uncle to translate. It read:

Dear friend and fellow Grail Knight,

You do not find the Grail.

The cup finds you.

Its treasure is in its mystery,

As you can see from its legends and history.

The Quest can take a lifetime, and the rewards are in the seeking.

A Grail Knight must be brave, truthful, and bold until the end.

Only then will your quest for the cup stop,

And the true Grail you will behold.

The Legend of the
HOLY GRAIL

The Holy Grail is closely connected to the legend of King Arthur. In medieval times, England was supposed to have been ruled by a great king named Arthur. King Arthur formed a group of special knights, and they became known as the Knights of the Round Table. Some of these knights went in search of the Grail because it was supposed to possess miraculous properties. It was believed that the Grail was held in a castle in the middle of a wasteland, and that it was guarded by someone known as the Fisher King. The knights who searched for the Grail became known as Grail Knights, and their quests became legendary stories. The tales of these brave knights have become the subject of many modern books, plays, and adventure movies.

Though many believe this cup does exist, it has never been found. Today, the symbol of the Holy Grail represents a commitment to a great lifetime quest.

enigma scyphi

Glossary

abbey a religious place where monks live

armor metal clothes worn to protect the body

cataloging writing a list in order to keep records

chamber a private room

crest a special symbol that stands for a particular group

decipher decode or work something out

engrossed fully absorbed by

goblet a drinking vessel with a foot and a stem

imposing making an impression due to great size or appearance

impressive worth taking note of; important

instincts feelings and urges which come from within a person

knight a man, usually of noble birth, who was a soldier

Latin an ancient language

legend a story handed down from the past

medieval from the Middle Ages; very old

monks men who have withdrawn from the world to join a religious order

parchment a type of thick paper; used to be made from animal skins

quest a search made to find a particular thing

stagnant stale; not moving

stoked poked and stirred up a fire

tapestry a picture made by sewing colored threads on canvas

theory a suggested explanation

vow of silence a promise not to speak or make any vocal sounds

Titles in This Series